MINUTE 2
MYSTERIES

MORE STORIES TO SOLVE

American Girl®

Published by Pleasant Company Publications
Copyright © 2007 by American Girl, LLC

Questions or comments? Call 1-800-845-0005,
visit our Web site at **americangirl.com**, or write to Customer Service,
American Girl, 8400 Fairway Place, Middleton, WI 53562-0497.

Printed in China
07 08 09 10 11 LEO 12 11 10 9 8 7 6 5 4 3 2 1

The image of the *S.S. Londonia* Morse code card (p. 61) appears
courtesy of becker&mayer! Card designed by J. Max Steinmetz.

Written by Teri Witkowski and Jennifer Hirsch
Designed by Justin King
Produced by Jeannette Bailey, Julie Kimmell, Gretchen Krause,
and Judith Lary
Illustrations by Dan Andreasen, Nick Backes, Bill Farnsworth,
Renée Graef, Susan McAliley, Walter Rane, Luann Roberts,
Keith Skeen, Dahl Taylor, and Jean-Paul Tibbles

Cataloging-in-Publication Data
available from the Library of Congress.

TABLE OF CONTENTS

Molly burst in the door and set her schoolbooks down on the kitchen table. Something smelled delicious. "What are you baking, Mrs. Gilford?" Molly asked.

"A new recipe for Boston brown bread, baked in a coffee can," said Mrs. Gilford. "Try a piece."

Eagerly, Molly picked up a piece. "This is delicious!" she said between bites. "And this reminds me—may I have your recipes for brownies and oatmeal cookies? Susan, Linda, and I are having a bake sale to raise money for the Red Cross."

"What a fine contribution to the war effort," Mrs. Gilford said with approval. She handed Molly the recipes. "Here you go. When you make your shopping list, don't forget to multiply the ingredients according to how many batches you plan to bake."

For the next several weeks, Molly, Linda, and Susan saved their allowances in a tin can

Molly's Bake Sale

that Linda had labeled "bake-sale fund." They also asked their families to save up their rations of butter, sugar, and eggs so that they would have enough to bake with.

On the day before the sale, Linda and Susan were to spend the night at Molly's house. In the afternoon, the three girls took the can, which was clanking with money, to the grocery store to buy the ingredients. After dinner, Molly's sister, Jill, helped them bake the brownies and oatmeal cookies.

"Mmm, these sure smell good," said Linda, taking another tray of cookies out of the oven.

Susan was slicing up pans of brownies, which had already cooled.

"Stop nibbling at the brownies, Susan,"said Molly. "We're selling them, remember?"

"I'm only eating the crumbs that come off on the knife," said Susan. "We can't sell those. And we wouldn't want them to go to waste, after spending all our allowance on the ingredients."

"Well, I guess," Molly agreed, helping herself to a large brownie crumb that had fallen off the knife onto the table. "Yum, these *are* good. How much should we charge?"

"It seems like we have a lot more cookies. The pans of brownies are smaller," Linda said. "So maybe we should charge more for the brownies."

Susan nodded. "The brownie ingredients were more expensive, too."

"And they taste the best, so probably more

people will want them," Molly pointed out. "How about a nickel for a cookie and a dime for a brownie?" Linda and Susan agreed.

The next day, the bake sale was a big success, and by noon the girls were tallying up their earnings.

"I can't believe it!" Linda exclaimed. "We made 180 cookies and brownies, and we sold every single one!"

Susan didn't look quite as delighted as Linda. "I never even got to eat one of the brownies," she mumbled.

"You got to eat lots of crumbs last night," Molly reminded her. "Besides, look how much money we made for the Red Cross!"

If the girls sold twice as many cookies as brownies, how much money did they make altogether? The answer is on page 62.

Addy was walking home from school on a day in early spring when she spotted her father driving the ice wagon. "Poppa!" Addy cried, racing down the street to meet him.

"Well, well," Poppa said in his deep voice. "Look what the wind blew my way. If you want a ride home, I'm going to be heading that way in a bit. I've got a few stops to make first."

Addy was happy to join Poppa on his deliveries. At each stop, she waited patiently while he exchanged pleasantries with the customers on his route. At his last stop, Poppa introduced Addy to a man named Mr. Franklin. Mr. Franklin knew Mr. and Mrs. Golden, the couple who ran the boarding house where Addy and her family lived.

"How are things at the Goldens'?" Mr. Franklin asked Addy.

"Just fine, sir," answered Addy. "Mr. Golden's mother moved in a few days ago."

8

"You don't say," replied Mr. Franklin. "Why, the last time I saw M'dear, she was at my cousin's house. Mr. Golden's sister had just had a baby that she named Abraham. M'dear was mighty proud of her new grandson. My mother told M'dear that she couldn't be the only one who got to hold that baby. Abraham is my mother's great-nephew, and she was determined to have that baby in her arms before the day was done!" Poppa and Addy laughed as Mr. Franklin described the women's good-natured argument. When it was time to head home, Mr. Franklin told Addy to say hello to M'dear for him.

Poppa looked puzzled when he climbed back into the wagon. "After all that, I'm not exactly sure how Mr. Franklin knows Mr. Golden," he said as he picked up the reins.

Addy grinned. "I do, Poppa. Mr. Franklin doesn't just know Mr. Golden. He's *related* to him!"

How are the two men related? Turn to page 62 to find out.

 Samantha was thrilled that Agnes and Agatha were spending the summer with her at Piney Point. Grandmary's home in the mountains was one of Samantha's favorite places, and the twins were two of Samantha's favorite people. The girls spent their days swimming, canoeing, and exploring the outdoors. The only thing that kept them inside was rain, and today it was coming down in a steady shower. Samantha suggested they set up their easels and paint on the porch. "That way we can be outdoors and not get wet," she explained.

It was a little windy on the porch and rather damp, but that didn't stop the three artists. They worked quietly until Agnes put down her brush and sighed heavily. "I'm having trouble making the paint go where I want it to go," she said crossly.

"Maybe there's something wrong with these paintbrushes," Agatha suggested. "Maybe they're worn out."

"Grandmary told me there are more brushes in the attic," said Samantha. "Let's go look for them." She led the way up the wide stairs to the second floor and then up the narrow steps to the attic.

"Oooh, look!" cried Agatha as though she'd found a treasure. "Old hats! Boxes and boxes of them!" The girls threw off the dusty lids and lifted the hats out of tissue paper. The hats were old-fashioned and frilly, and the girls giggled as they tried them on. As they explored the rest of the attic, Samantha found a box of photo albums and scrapbooks. The gold-edged pages looked as if no one had turned them in a long, long time.

Samantha sat on the floor and opened one of the heavy books. The pictures were brown and yellow, and a little faded.

"What is that?" asked Agatha. She sat down next to Samantha.

"It's one of Grandmary's old photograph albums," answered Samantha. "Here's a picture of Grandpa."

Who's That Man?

"He was very dashing," Agnes said. She was peering over Samantha's shoulder. "When was that photograph taken?"

Samantha recognized Grandmary's graceful penmanship on the page next to the photograph. "There's no date, but Grandmary wrote 'Mr. Edwards's family, London, England.' Oh, this must have been taken shortly after they met," Samantha said excitedly. "Their courtship was very romantic. They met just a month before Grandpa went to England for a year. They wrote a letter to each other every single week. When Grandpa came back to America, they became engaged. They were married two years later."

The last photograph in the album was of Grandmary in her wedding gown. It was dated June 10, 1867.

"How elegant!" Agnes sighed. Agatha and Samantha agreed.

When Samantha lifted the heavy book off

her lap, a loose photograph fell to the floor. Agatha picked it up, glanced at it, and handed it to Samantha. "It's someone else's wedding, but your grandparents are there," she said.

Samantha studied the picture. Grandmary stood next to the bride, and next to her was a man whose face was partially hidden by his hat. Grandmary's hand rested on the man's arm, and there was a smile on her face. Samantha turned the photograph over, but the only thing written on it was "1863." Samantha turned the photograph over again and looked at the man for a long time. "I don't know who this is," she finally said. "But I know it's not Grandpa." Samantha was grinning when she looked up at Agatha and Agnes. "I think Grandmary had another beau!"

Why was Samantha so certain the man in the photograph was not her grandpa? The answer is on page 62.

Felicity popped a sun-warmed strawberry into her mouth and smiled as the sweet, tangy juice ran over her tongue. It tasted of summertime. Felicity loved summer on Grandfather's plantation. Picking strawberries was work, but it wasn't the tedious, tiresome sort, like stitching a sampler. It was more like finding treasure. Each time Felicity lifted a crown of leaves to find a ripe red berry hiding underneath, she felt a little thrill.

"Lissie! Have you filled your basket yet? Or are you filling your belly instead?" Mother called from the garden path.

Felicity laughed. "Indeed, it's tempting to eat them all, but I don't think I'd have room!" She stood up and brought the nearly full basket to Mother, who handed her two empty ones.

"This one is for you, and the other is for Nan and William, when they finish filling their first basket," said Mother.

"*If* they finish," said Felicity. The last time

16

she had checked on her brother and sister, who were four and seven years old, their mouths were bright red and their basket nearly empty.

"Just remind them that there'll be no strawberry pie at supper if they eat all their berries now," Mother said with a smile.

Felicity set her basket beside an unpicked row and made her way around a large trellis of climbing peas to the other end of the strawberry patch, where Nan and William were. Nan appeared to be picking steadily, but William was crouched in the dirt between the rows, peering at the ground.

"Have you found a nice June bug, William?" Felicity asked. Her little brother was fascinated by beetles, caterpillars, and creepy-crawlies of all sorts.

William shook his head. "Handprints. Little ones. Look!" He pointed a strawberry-stained finger at the ground.

Felicity and Nan looked down. Sure enough, a row of tiny handprints was neatly outlined in the soft soil.

The Pie Thief

"What dainty little prints!" said Nan. "Who would have such tiny hands?"

"Maybe it was elves!" William whispered, his eyes round.

Nan giggled. "Elves walking on their hands!"

Felicity smiled. "I think it was raccoons. They come out at night and climb into the garden. They like the strawberries too! Now, let's finish our picking so that we can have strawberry pie at supper."

William's eyes lit up. "My favorite! I can't wait. Oh, I love strawberry pie more than anything!"

"Well, there won't be any if we don't get back to work," said Felicity.

"And you musn't eat all the berries you pick, William," Nan added.

The three children went back to the strawberry patch and picked for the rest of the morning. William ate a great many strawberries, and Nan and Felicity ate a few just to keep their strength up, but finally they had three full baskets to bring to Mother.

In the afternoon, William napped while Felicity and Nan played by the river. The girls built a sand castle and watched muskrats swimming in the shallows. When they returned, there were two golden pies set to cool on the windowsill of the summer kitchen.

"Ooh, Lissie, don't those pies look delicious!" said Nan. "I'm so hungry, I could eat a whole one right now."

"So could I," laughed Felicity. "But that wouldn't leave any pie for anyone else! Come on, let's go wash up and dress for supper."

Supper was served in Grandfather's elegant dining room. As Felicity came in, Mary, the house servant, was drawing the curtains against the rays of late-afternoon sunlight that slanted through the windows. That was another thing Felicity loved about summer— the long daylight that lingered well past supper. She took a deep breath as she sat down. Roast pheasant—it smelled delicious.

"I'm starving!" said Nan as everyone began eating. "What's the matter, William? Aren't you hungry?"

Her little brother shrugged.

"Perhaps he's saving room for pie," said Felicity.

"You must eat your supper, William, if you want to have dessert," Mother reminded him. William shrugged again and picked at his food.

At last the dishes were cleared and the dessert plates set out. Felicity looked up in anticipation as Mary came bustling into the room with the pies. But Mary looked distraught.

"Look here!" Mary exclaimed. "Something, or someone, has gone and eaten the better part of one of my pies!" She set the pies on the table before Grandfather. Sure enough, one of them was missing most of its middle. Red juice pooled in the collapsed center, where the other pie had a woven crown of crust.

"Well, well," said Grandfather. "A pie thief." He looked sternly around the table and settled his gaze on Felicity. "As the eldest child and chief strawberry picker, have you any knowledge of this matter?"

Felicity shook her head. "No, Grandfather. When Nan and I came in from the river, the pies were cooling on the windowsill of the summer kitchen. Nothing had touched them."

"I think they'd just come out of the oven," Nan added.

"I see." Grandfather looked around the table at William, Mother, and Mary. "Does anyone else have anything to say?"

"I know what it was!" William exclaimed.

Grandfather raised his bushy eyebrows. "Indeed? Pray tell us what you know, lad."

"It was the raccoons! The same ones who were stealing strawberries in the garden." He turned to his sisters. "Remember those handprints we saw?"

"Yes!" Nan cried indignantly. "Those cheeky little beasts! It's not enough for them to take our strawberries, they must ruin our pie, too?"

Felicity shook her head. "I don't think the pie is completely ruined, actually," she began.

"Well, I'm not eating any," Nan declared. "Not if those nasty raccoons have been digging around in it with their dirty little hands!"

"That's just the point," Felicity cut in. "I don't think it was raccoon hands at all!"

What was Felicity thinking? Turn to page 63 to find out.

"Come with me, boys. I have a surprise to show you," Kaya called as she pulled a warm deerskin robe around her shoulders. In this cold season, Kaya's mother often asked her to take her twin brothers out of the smoky, crowded longhouse for fresh air and exercise. Sparrow and Wing Feather were in their fifth winter, and they were always eager to go exploring with Kaya.

"What is the surprise, Kaya?" Wing Feather asked as they crossed the winter village.

Kaya smiled. "Something you will like. Wait and see."

Suddenly, Kaya felt a tug on her braid. A boy named Fox Tail, who liked to tease Kaya, fell into step with them. "Wait and see what?" he asked.

"Kaya's taking us to a surprise!" Sparrow said excitedly. "Do you want to come along?"

Oh, dear, thought Kaya. *This bothersome boy will pester me all afternoon if he comes along.* But

24

before she could say anything, Fox Tail shook his head.

"I have more important things to do," he answered. "Besides, I don't think Kaya's surprise will be anything special." He gave Kaya's braid another tug and then turned and walked toward the river.

"It will *too* be special," Wing Feather called after Fox Tail.

"Never mind him," Kaya said, relieved that Fox Tail was heading in the opposite direction. "Come on, let's run!" She led the boys up into the foothills above the village, their fur-lined moccasins leaving faint tracks in the frost-covered grass. They climbed up a steep slope and into a thicket of shrub willows. When the boys were settled next to her, Kaya pushed the branches back to create an opening they could peer through.

The boys gasped happily when they saw the pond below. A beaver lodge, shaped like a squat tepee, sat on one side of the pond. Ripples marked the blue surface of the water as a large

beaver swam back and forth in front of the
lodge.

"*Tawts!*" Sparrow said in a hushed voice.
"Good. The surprise is a beaver!"

"A family of beavers!" Kaya whispered.

"That's the one I call Old Scout."

Another large beaver surfaced outside the lodge and swam about in front of it. "That's Old Scout's mate," Kaya said. "I call her Brings a Branch because she's so good at felling trees."

Right behind Brings a Branch, two other beavers swam out of the underwater entrance-way to the lodge. They were lighter in color and smaller than the two adults. "Those are their kits," Kaya whispered. "I call them Dip and Dive. They want to play all the time, just like you two!"

The boys were delighted with the surprise. They held back giggles as they watched Dip and Dive play in front of the lodge. The young beavers dove and surfaced in unison and slid over each other with soft splashes, like river otters. "We're like Dip and Dive!" Wing Feather said with a grin. "Look, they swim right toward each other and dive just before they crash." He shoved Sparrow with his shoulder, and his twin shoved back.

Kaya and her brothers watched the antics

in the pond until their cheeks grew numb from the cold. The boys didn't want to leave, but Kaya promised to bring them back again soon.

When they returned to the village, they met Fox Tail going into the entrance of the longhouse. "You should have come with us," Sparrow announced. "Kaya's surprise was a good one."

"We saw a beaver pond," Wing Feather added. "And there were—"

Fox Tail interrupted. "I had work to do," he said. His cheeks were bright red, and his breath hung in white puffs in the cold air. "I've been inside all day mending my fishing nets. I'm not interested in a silly beaver family."

"Oh, no?" Kaya teased. She pulled the heavy buffalo hide back from the entrance to the lodge, and the boys scurried in to warm themselves by the fire. "Maybe next time you'll walk with us instead of following us."

What made Kaya think Fox Tail had followed them? Turn to page 62 for the answer.

Kit, Ruthie, and Stirling were working on a new issue of *The Hard Times News.*

True, their newspaper office was really a bedroom, and the reporters, who were all recovering from scarlet fever, were dressed in pajamas. But Kit still took the job of newspaper writing very seriously.

"We should make a crossword puzzle for people to do," said Stirling. "Like real newspapers have."

"This is a real newspaper," Kit said sharply. "We provide real news."

"Okay, okay, you know what I mean. A newspaper that *grownups* read."

"Grownups read my newspaper!" Kit was indignant.

"He means grownups who aren't your parents," Ruthie explained.

"All the boarders read my newspaper. They're grownups, and they certainly aren't my parents!" Kit was almost shouting.

"I mean a newspaper that people have to

pay for," Stirling cut in quickly. "Calm down, Kit. Of course this is a real newspaper. But it would be even more real if it had a crossword puzzle."

"Well, I don't know," Kit said. "I'm pretty busy writing *real* articles." Secretly, she thought

a crossword puzzle was a good idea. But
she was still smarting at the notion that her
newspaper was just play, so she didn't want
to admit that the idea was a good one.

"That's a great idea!" said Ruthie. "I love
doing crossword puzzles. How about if I make
it? I mean, since you're busy doing the articles,"
she added quickly with a nervous glance
at Kit.

"Well . . ." Kit hesitated. "Okay. But make
sure it has lots of big words, not just a bunch of
little easy ones. Remember, this is a newspaper
for grownups."

Ruthie and Stirling flushed. Stirling handed
Ruthie a pencil and then turned back to the
illustration he was drawing.

Half an hour later, Ruthie was still bent over
her paper, hard at work. Creating a crossword
puzzle wasn't easy. "Can anyone think of a
word that has four G's in it?" she asked.

Kit paused in her typing. "How many letters
should it have?"

"Eight."

"What letter does it need to start with?" Stirling asked.

"G," said Ruthie.

"And what letter should it end with?" asked Kit.

"G," said Ruthie. "Never mind. I think it's impossible."

Suddenly Kit began to laugh.

"What's so funny?" asked Stirling.

"The word I thought of!" Kit answered.

What was it? The answer is on page 62.

The streets of Maryville were crowded when Papa stopped the wagon across from Mr. Berkhoff's store. "Kirsten, look!" Peter cried. "Everyone's here for the Fourth of July." Kirsten had never seen Maryville so bustling with buggies and wagons and people. The little park in the center of town was filled with families from neighboring farms. Everyone was gathering for the music, games, and big parade.

"Before the fun, there's work to do," Papa said as Kirsten and Peter scrambled out of the wagon. Papa and Lars started to unpack crates filled with homemade sausages, cheese, and jelly. They were going to sell the items to Mr. Berkhoff in exchange for the things they needed on the farm.

Kirsten stood next to the wagon, trying to be patient. She was aching to race into the store and look at all the treasures and finery. Peter *was* racing. He ran around the wagon, zig-zagging between Lars and Papa as they tried to unpack the crates.

"Peter, stop!" Mama scolded. "You're going to run into someone. Kirsten, will you take Peter inside the store and—"

Before Mama could finish, Peter and Kirsten were running across the dirt road.

"Be careful," Mama called after Kirsten. "And keep an eye on your brother."

The little store hummed as loudly as a beehive with the voices of shoppers. Kirsten took a deep breath. She smelled the mouth-watering scent of spices and coffee. Before she could decide where to start, Peter tugged at her dress.

"I want to look at pocketknives," he announced. "It won't hurt just to look, will it?"

Kirsten grinned. "Pretend you can have any knife you want," she said. "Pretending won't hurt." She took Peter's hand and began to steer him carefully through the crowd, but her eager brother bumped into a tall, lanky man in a white coat and yellow bow tie.

"Pardon me, sir," Kirsten said shyly. She had never seen the man before.

The man smiled. "That's quite all right, young miss. The store is mighty busy today, isn't it?"

"It sure is!" Peter loudly agreed.

"Hush, Peter," Kirsten scolded. It didn't seem polite to talk so boldly to a stranger, but the man looked jolly. He had a thin mustache that turned up at the ends, even when he wasn't smiling.

"And who is this anxious fellow with you?" the man asked.

"This is my brother, Peter," answered Kirsten.

"We're going to look at pocketknives," Peter announced.

"A fine thing to look at," agreed the man. "You're lucky to have a big sister to keep an eye on you," the man said, looking at Peter. "When I was growing up, I was the only child in my family. It sure was lonesome." Then the man looked around the bustling store. "On a day like this, with so many folks around—well, there can't be a lonely soul for miles and miles. You two have a nice time today."

"Thank you, sir," Kirsten answered as Peter pulled her toward the display of knives. They studied the glass case for a long time before Kirsten could coax Peter into exploring the rest of the store. As they were admiring the jars of hard candy on the counter, Mr. Berkhoff appeared.

"Hello, you two," he said with a smile. "Your friend just bought you each a piece of candy. What would you like?"

"Wow!" Peter exclaimed.

But Kirsten was puzzled. "Our friend?" she asked.

"The gentleman in the yellow bow tie. He knew Peter here by name." Mr. Berkhoff nodded at the man in the white coat who was carrying a box of supplies out of the store. "He asked me to put two pieces of candy on his bill," Mr. Berkhoff explained. "He said his brother was on his way into the store to pick

out a new ax and would pay for everything at once."

"Kirsten, can I really choose a piece of candy?" Peter asked. He was hopping excitedly from one foot to the other.

"No, Peter," Kirsten said firmly. "That would be stealing." Then she looked at Mr. Berkhoff. "That man is stealing, too, Mr. Berkhoff. He's going to take those things without paying for them. You have to stop him!"

Why did Kirsten think the man was a thief? Find out on page 63.

Josefina and her sisters bustled about the crowded kitchen. There was a lot to do to get ready for that night's *fiesta*, and the girls chatted excitedly as they worked. The Montoyas always hosted a big party to celebrate the Feast of the Three Kings, which was the last day of the Christmas season.

"Everything smells delicious," Tía Dolores announced as she polished the hot-chocolate pot. "Our guests will enjoy all the fine food you are making, and your papá will be proud of how hard you girls are working."

"*Gracias*," Ana answered as she filled turnover dough with fruit. "But we could not have done so well without you." Tía Dolores had come to the *rancho* a few months ago to help the girls after their mamá had died a year earlier. This was the first fiesta Tía Dolores had prepared with them, and all the girls were grateful for their aunt's sensible guidance and her cheerful encouragement.

Tía Dolores went to the fire and stirred the

big pot of spicy chile stew. "That may be so," she said. "But you girls were very fine cooks before I arrived. Your mamá taught you well."

Josefina's face was warm from the heat of the fire and from her aunt's praise. "Mamá loved fiestas," Josefina said as she tied a cornhusk wrapping around a meat-filled tamale. "It has been fun to make all the special treats she made every year."

"Especially *bizcochito* cookies," Francisca said, pressing her fists into a large ball of bread dough. "Those were Mamá's favorites."

Tía Dolores smiled. "*Si.* Your mamá loved those cookies when we were little girls. But surely she was not the only one in your family to like bizcochitos, was she?" Tía Dolores teased.

"Oh, no," said Josefina with a grin. "Someone else likes bizcochitos very much. Isn't that right, Clara?"

Clara, who was kneeling on the floor grinding corn into coarse flour, was usually very sensible and serious. But when she saw the mischievous look in Josefina's eyes, she grinned, too. "Si," she answered mysteriously. "There are three family members who like sweet treats."

"But Clara's not one of them," Ana said, playing along.

"Clara's favorite treat is spicy," Josefina said.

"But not as spicy as Francisca's favorite," Clara added. "Francisca is especially fond of chiles."

"And Ana is especially fond of what she is making," Francisca chimed in.

"Remember that Josefina does not *eat* her favorite treat," Ana said.

Josefina started to giggle, and soon everyone was laughing. "All right, you clever girls," Tía Dolores said. "I think I've figured out your riddle. I may even know who likes bizcochitos as much as your mamá did!"

What did Tía Dolores guess was each person's favorite treat? Fill out the chart below, and then turn to page 62 to check your answers.

Treat	Person
tamales	
chile stew	
hot chocolate	
fruit turnovers	
bizcochitos	

"Would you like another cookie, Emily?" Molly asked, holding out a plate of peanut butter cookies to her new friend. Emily was from England, and three weeks earlier she had traveled by ship, all by herself, to America to be safe. London, where she usually lived, was being bombed because of the war.

Emily looked up from the letter she was writing to her parents, who were still in London. "I'm sorry?" she asked with a bewildered look on her face. It wasn't until she saw the plate Molly was holding that she understood. "Oh, a biscuit. Yes, thank you," she said politely, taking the smallest cookie.

Molly giggled. "I forgot that you call them *biscuits*," she said warmly. Molly and Emily had been shy with each other at first, but now they were getting to be good friends.

"And I forgot to tell Mum and Dad that Americans call them *cookies*," Emily said.

Even though British and Americans both

spoke English, it seemed to Emily that they spoke different kinds of English. There were different names for things, like *cookies* for biscuits, *sweater* for jumper, and *sneakers* for plimsolls. When Molly had shown Emily her nurse doll, Emily told Molly that in England, women who work in hospitals were called *sisters*. Nurses, Emily explained, took care of little children.

"Things must seem kind of strange here," Molly said sympathetically.

"Quite," Emily agreed. "I was just writing to my parents about all I've learned since I arrived."

"Did you tell them about all the milk?" Molly asked.

Now Emily giggled. "Indeed!" Emily had been shocked to find that milk was not as carefully rationed in America. She had practically stared at Ricky the first morning he poured milk on his oatmeal. He used twice as much as an entire day's milk ration in England!

"I learned in school that your rationing in

England is lots stricter than ours is here," said Molly. "You couldn't have hardly any meat or eggs or fruit or—"

"Milk!" the girls said in unison.

"And," Emily explained, "most of those things are hardly ever in the shops anyway. You can't get them even if you have ration points and plenty of money. Meat is especially scarce. Here," she said, handing Molly the letter she'd just received from her mother. "Mum wrote about waiting for hours at the butcher shop."

Molly read the part of the letter Emily was pointing to. "What's q-u-e-u-e?" Molly asked.

Now it was her turn to look bewildered.

"It's *queue*," Emily explained, pronouncing the word like the letter Q. "You call it a line. Word got out that the butcher had meat, so everyone stood in line hoping to get some."

All Molly could think to say was "gosh." Her family had to save and trade ration stamps to buy the food they needed, but they didn't have to stand in line to buy meat, and they had never gone without milk. "I think you're very brave, Emily," Molly finally said.

"Oh, no," Emily said quickly. "I'm not. If I were brave, I wouldn't be so scared about the Flutophone performance on Saturday."

Molly and Emily's third-grade class had been given Flutophones on loan. They had been learning to play the clarinet-like instruments, and they were going to perform "America the Beautiful" in front of the whole school at the PTA program. Their teacher, Miss Campbell, had selected Emily to play a solo. Emily was very nervous. She simply hated the idea of being the center of attention, especially since she was not a very good Flutophone player.

"You'll be fine," Molly reassured her friend. "You've been practicing like crazy, and Linda and Susan and I will be right behind you onstage."

Emily looked a little bit relieved at that thought. "Right-oh," she said as bravely as she could. "I won't be completely alone. That would be simply dreadful."

★

On Friday afternoon, Miss Campbell took the class to the auditorium to rehearse their performance. When the students were seated onstage, Miss Campbell explained that she would introduce the class and then open the curtain. "Here's your cue, Emily," Miss Campbell said, pulling a rope on the side of the stage that opened the heavy red curtains. "Here's where you begin."

Emily was still nervous about her solo, but now she was confused, too. "By the curtain?"

she asked. "I'm to play there?"

"No," Miss Campbell answered. "You'll stand in the center of the stage."

"I see," Emily answered. The fluttery feeling in her stomach was getting worse. "All right then." Emily straightened her shoulders and raised the Flutophone to her lips.

"Your cue is the curtain, Emily," Susan whispered helpfully.

Emily felt her face flush hot with confusion. She lowered the Flutophone and walked to the side of the stage where Miss Campbell stood. Emily took a deep breath to try to calm herself, again raised the instrument to her lips, and began to shakily play the first few notes of "America the Beautiful." She didn't get very far before she heard the confused murmurs of her classmates and felt Miss Campbell's hand on her shoulder.

"Just a moment, Emily," Miss Campbell gently interrupted. "This isn't quite right."

Emily stopped playing and looked like she was about to start crying. "I don't understand," she said, her voice quivering.

"I do!" Molly said with a start. She jumped up from her chair and hurried to where her friend stood. "Emily is right, Miss Campbell. You did ask her to stand over here."
Now Miss Campbell looked confused.
"I did?" she asked.

"Yes," Molly said, putting a reassuring arm around Emily. "She did exactly what you asked."

What did Molly mean? The answer is on page 63.

Kit stepped out onto the back porch and took a deep breath of sun-warmed air. It was early June, and Mother's flowers were in bloom! Now that the house was full of boarders, Mother didn't have as much time to work in her garden. But that didn't stop the flowers from growing. The daffodils and crocuses had been the first to poke through the ground. Then the azalea bush blossomed. Now pink snapdragons, white daisies, and red peonies were blooming. The deep purple irises—Kit's favorite—stood proudly in the center of the flower bed. Kit couldn't help but smile. Even though the Depression had changed so much in their lives, Mother's flowers still filled the backyard with bursts of color.

The back door opened and Mother came out, carrying her garden gloves and the morning mail. "Is there a letter from Charlie?" Kit asked. Charlie was in Montana working for the Civilian Conservation Corps, and Kit eagerly awaited each letter from her brother.

"Not today, dear," her mother answered. "But there is a letter from Mrs. Wolf. It seems she's in charge of organizing the garden show this year."

"Are you going to help with the show?" Kit asked.

"Actually, Mrs. Wolf has invited me to enter the competition," Mother said.

"That's wonderful," Kit exclaimed, expecting her mother to be happy.

Instead, Mother sighed and folded the letter. "I haven't had time to properly tend to the flowers," Mother explained. She looked at the corner of the lawn that Aunt Millie had turned into a vegetable patch. That was the only gardening Mother had time for now.

Mother put the letter from Mrs. Wolf into the pocket of her apron and picked up her gloves. "There's no sense in thinking about the garden show. Let's see how those carrots are coming along." She smiled at Kit, but it wasn't the eager smile she used to wear when she headed to the garden.

"Wait!" Kit cried, following her mother down the steps. "I have an idea. Let me take care of the vegetables so that you'll have time to get your flowers ready for the show."

"That's kind of you, dear," Mother said without stopping. "But you already have so many chores to do."

"But school is out," Kit reasoned as they crossed the yard. "The Bells have left, which means there are fewer dishes to wash and one less bed to change. You see? I have time to help!" By the time they'd reached the edge of the vegetable patch, Kit knew that her mother was considering the idea.

"Well," Mother said, looking over at the flowerbeds. "The rain we've had *does* have all of the flowers off to a fine start." Mother's eyes went from the irises to the snapdragons to the daisies. She was arranging a vase of flowers in her head. Kit just knew it!

"The vegetables won't be ready to pick until *after* the garden show," Kit reminded her mother. "There's plenty of time."

Mother smiled, and this time it was one of her real smiles that made Kit feel like smiling, too. "Kit Kittredge, you are a determined girl! How can I say no to all your help? All right, I *will* enter the competition."

During the next few weeks, Kit and Mother spent their mornings in the garden. Kit weeded and watered the vegetable patch. Mother did the same in her flowerbeds where she carefully inspected each leaf and petal.

When the morning of the show arrived, Mother spent a long time in the garden. She cut the best flowers and gently placed the stems in a bucket of water. Then Mrs. Smithens drove her to the exhibition hall. Mother would be arranging the flowers there and entering them in the Cut Flowers category.

"I can't wait to see Mother's arrangement," Kit told Ruthie as the two of them walked downtown later that day. "I just know they'll be the most beautiful flowers there."

The exhibit hall was enormous, and it was filled with every kind of flower and plant imaginable. Cards in front of each pot listed the name of the plant and the grower. Ruthie decided the lilies were her favorite, and Kit learned that the sweet-smelling flower she liked most was a gardenia.

In the Cut Flowers section, the arrangements were displayed in vases, baskets, pitchers, bowls, buckets, and even teacups. Many of the bouquets included the same kinds of flowers Kit's mother grew.

"Gosh, I thought I'd be able to spot Mother's arrangement right away," Kit confessed to Ruthie. "Now I'm not so sure I can tell which flowers came from my own backyard!"

Kit had just started reading the names on the cards in front of each bouquet when she heard someone call her name. It was Mrs. Wolf.

"Hello, Mrs. Wolf," Kit said politely. "Do you remember my friend, Ruth Ann Smithens?"

What's Growing On?

"Yes, of course. Hello," Mrs. Wolf answered. "Kit, dear, I'm so pleased you convinced your mother to enter. Her arrangement is exquisite."

Kit's face broke out into a broad grin. "Oh, I knew it would be. We haven't seen it yet."

"It's right over here. I'll show you." Mrs. Wolf led the girls to the next aisle. "Your mother's irises are the prettiest pale blue," she said, stopping in front of a tall crystal vase. "And the yellow daisies are such a fine complement. Your mother has such a good eye."

"Oh, Kit. They're lovely!" Ruthie exclaimed. But Kit was not smiling.

"Yes, these are beautiful," Kit said, picking up the card with her mother's name on it. "But they're not my mother's flowers. Mrs. Wolf, this card is in front of the wrong bouquet!"

If Kit hadn't seen her mother's bouquet, how could she know that the arrangement Mrs. Wolf showed her was the wrong one? Turn to page 63 to find out.

Dots and Dashes

April 20, 1906
Dear Nellie,

Traveling on an ocean liner is
even more splendid than I imagined.
Everything is so elegant. Grandmary
and I had tea in the Ocean Garden, which
is like a tropical forest. There are ferns and
orchids everywhere. I also visited the library,
which has more than 1,000 books. It would take
a very long trip to read all of them!

The Admiral showed me the radio room
where telegraphs are sent and received. I got to
see the wireless operator tap out the letters in
Morse code using dots and dashes. The wireless operator gave me two Morse code cards, so
I'm sending one to you. If we both practice, we
can send messages in code.

The most exciting part of the trip happened
last night. The Captain invited the Admiral,
Grandmary, and me to join him for dinner.
Sitting at the Captain's Table is the highest
honor, and the Grand Dining Salon is

beautiful. The ceiling is made entirely out of stained glass, and Grandmary said the table-cloths were made of *imported* lace. There were so many courses that it took us nearly three hours to finish eating.

Nellie, I just had a fun idea! I'll send you the dinner menu in Morse code, and you can use the code card to read it. We'll become Morse code experts.

I will mail this letter to you when we arrive in England. Grandmary says you'll receive it before we get back to New York. That will give you time to decode the dinner menu. I can't wait to tell you all about the rest of my trip when I return.

I miss you!

Love, Samantha

Turn the page to see the dinner menu Samantha sent to Nellie. Use the code card and write down the letter that corresponds to the combination of dots and dashes. The / symbol separates two different words. Check your answers on page 63.

```
---   -•--  •••  -  •  •-•  •••
 o     y     s   t  e   r    s
```

1 ••• --- ••- •--•

2 ••• •- •-•• -- --- -•

3 -•-• •••• •• -•-• -•- • -•

4 •-• --- •- ••• -/

-•• ••- -•-• -•- •-•• •• -• --•

5 ••• •• •-• •-•• --- •• -•/

--- ••-• / -••• • • ••-•

6 --• •-• • • -• / •--• • •- •••

7 -•-• •-• • •- -- • -••/

-•-• •- •-• •-• --- - •••

Dots and Dashes

8 •-• •• -•-• •

9 -- •- ••• •••• • -••/

•--• --- - •- - --- • •••

10 •--• • •- -•-• •••• • •••

11 •• -•-• • / -•-• •-• • •- --

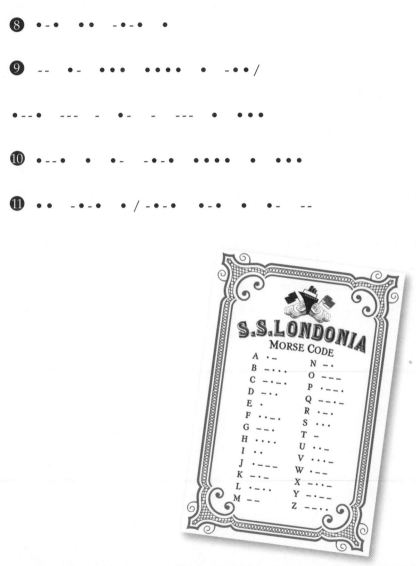

S.S. LONDONIA
MORSE CODE

A •—
B —•••
C —•—•
D —••
E •
F ••—•
G ——•
H ••••
I ••
J •———
K —•—
L •—••
M ——

N —•
O ———
P •——•
Q ——•—
R •—•
S •••
T —
U ••—
V •••—
W •——
X —••—
Y —•——
Z ——••

WHO'S THAT MAN?

Samantha knew that her grandparents married in 1867. They had met just before Mr. Edwards went to England for a year. When he returned to the United States, they were engaged for two years. Samantha did the math and determined that they met in 1864. The loose photograph was dated 1863—a year before Grandmary and Grandpa met!

Giggling

AN EIGHT-LETTER MYSTERY

SECRET TREATS

tamales: Clara
chile stew: Francisca
hot chocolate: Josefina
fruit turnovers: Ana
bizcochitos: Papá

CLUES IN THE COLD

Kaya suspected that Fox Tail had been outside for a while because his cheeks were red from the cold. She knew he had followed them to the pond when he mentioned the beaver family. Fox Tail couldn't have known there was more than one beaver unless he had been at the pond and seen them himself.

MOLLY'S BAKE SALE

$12.00, which was a lot of money in 1944! The girls sold 180 treats. Since there were twice as many cookies as brownies, there were 120 cookies and 60 brownies. Cookies cost a nickel, so 120 x 5 cents = 600 cents, or 6 dollars. Brownies cost a dime, and 60 x 10 cents = 600 cents, or 6 dollars.

IT'S ALL RELATIVE

Mr. Golden's mother is Abraham's grandmother. Mr. Franklin's mother is Abraham's great-aunt. That makes the two women sisters and the two men cousins.

Dots and Dashes

1. soup
2. salmon
3. chicken
4. roast duckling
5. sirloin of beef
6. green peas
7. creamed carrots
8. rice
9. mashed potatoes
10. peaches
11. ice cream

What's Growing On?

Kit's mother grew white daisies and deep purple irises in her garden. The arrangement Mrs. Wolf showed Kit included pale blue irises and yellow daisies. As soon as Kit saw the colors, she knew there was some kind of mix-up.

The Pie Thief

Felicity knew that raccoons are nocturnal—they come out only at night. They wouldn't have come to the summer kitchen in broad daylight. Based on the fact that William didn't seem hungry and had a ready excuse for the theft, Felicity figured that the pie thief must be William. She was right.

Trouble in Town

The man in the white coat told Mr. Berkhoff that his brother was going to pay for the supplies. But the man had told Kirsten and Peter that he was an only child. He didn't have a brother who would pay for his supplies.

The Confusing Cue

When Miss Campbell said, "Here's your cue," Emily thought her teacher had said "queue." That's why Emily went to stand by the curtain. She was getting into queue, and she was confused about why she had to line up, all by herself, by the curtain.